More Rawhides

More Rawhides

CHARLES M. RUSSELL

COMMONWEALTH BOOK COMPANY

1946 PREFACE

Of the three best known of our modern-day American story tellers, Charlie Russell, Irvin Cobb and Will Rogers, it was my good fortune to have heard the latter two. If one is to believe first-hand listener reports, Charlie Russell was the equal, if not the superior member, of the triumvirate. Will Rogers, great friend that he was of the Montana genius, insisted that "I always did say that you could tell a story better than any man that ever lived." Will Crawford, himself an artist-humorist of the old *Life* and *Judge* days, declared that the story-telling marathon at Charlie's birthday dinner in New York in 1904 (the story telling by Will Rogers and Charlie Russell lasted all night) ended in a dead heat. At that time Will Rogers was telling 'em on the stage with the Follies and Russell was trying to make a living as an artist and illustrator.

Cobb was a friend of the artist in the late years of Russell's life, and what a "pair to draw to" those two must have been!

In 1921 the first published booklet of Russell's salty cowboy stories, illustrated by the artist, was published by the local press of his home town, Great Falls, Montana. It was titled "Rawhide Rawlins Stories." In 1925 this was followed by another booklet of the same calibre which he named simply "More Rawhides." It is this rare little booklet that we now take pride in republishing. The many admirers of the greatest of all Western Artists may now enjoy another of his varied talents.

Trail's End
Pasadena, California.
July 27, 1946.

A few words about myself:
The papers have been kint to me,
many times more kind than true.
Altho I worked for many years
on the range, I am not what the
people think a cow boy should be
I was nsither a good roper nor
rider I was a night wrangler
how good I was I leave for the people
I worked for to say, thair are still
a few of them living.

In the spring I wrangled horses, in
the Fall I might heardid beef.
I worked for the big outfits
and always held my job.
I have many friends among
Cow men and cow punchers.
I have always been what is called a good
mixer — I had friends when I had
nothing Else. My friends were not
always within the law

*A page of Russell's original manuscript
from MORE RAWHIDES*

Table of Contents

A Few Words About Myself:

THE PAPERS have been kind to me,—many times more kind than true. Although I worked for many years on the range. I am not what the people think a cowboy should be. I was neither a good roper nor rider. I was a night wrangler. How good I was, I'll leave it for the people I worked for to say—there are still a few of them living. In the spring I wrangled horses—In the fall I herded beef. I worked for the big outfits and always held my job.

I have many friends among cowmen and cowpunchers. I have always been what is called a good mixer—I had friends when I had nothing else. My friends were not always within the law, but I haven't said how law-abiding I was myself. I haven't been too bad nor too good to get along with.

Life has never been too serious with me—I lived to play and I'm playing yet. Laughs and good judgment have saved me many a black eye but I don't laugh at other's tears. I was a wild young man but age has made me gentle. I drank, but never alone and when I drank it was no secret. I am still friendly with drinking men.

My friends are mixed—preachers, priests and sinners. I beiong to no church, but am friendly toward and respect all of them. I have always liked horses and since I was eight years old have always owned a few.

I am old-fashioned and peculiar in my dress. I am eccentric (that is a polite way of saying, you're crazy). I believe in luck and have had lots of it.

To have talent is no credit to its owner for what man can't help, he should get neither credit nor blame—it's not his fault. I am an illustrator. There are lots better ones, but some worse. Any man that can make a living doing what he likes is lucky, and I'm that. Any time I cash in now, I win.

--CHARLES M. RUSSELL
Great Falls, Montana

Right then's where the ball opens. 'Tain't so bad till they strike the sage brush country. Then, first one an' then another bounces by Bill's head.

Bullard's Wolves

LOTS OF cowpunchers like to play with a rope, but ropes, like guns, are dangerous. All the difference is guns go off and ropes go on. So you'll savvy my meanin', I'll tell you a story.

One time Bill Bullard's jogging along toward camp when he bumps into a couple of wolves that's been agin a bait. They've got enough strichnine so they're stiff and staggerin'. Bill drops his loop on one easy. Then he thinks. "What's the matter with taking both?" So he puts a couple of half hitches in the middle of his string, drops 'em over the horn, builds a loop at the other end of his rope, and dabs it on the second wolf. He's snaking 'em along all right till one of these calf-killers bumps on a sagebrush and bounces too near his hoss.

Right then's when the ball opens. The old hoss will stand anything but he don't like the smell of these meat eaters, so when this one starts crowdin' him, snappin' his teeth, he goes hog-wild, and wherever he's goin', Bill don't know, but the gait he takes, it's a cinch they won't be late. Tain't so bad till they hit the sagebrush country. Then, first one and then another bounces by Bill's head and lands ahead of them. This old cayuse starts trying to out-dodge this couple. Mr. Bullard manages to keep this cayuse headed for the camp, but he's mighty busy staying in the middle of this living lightning, he's riding.

When the boys in camp see him coming down the bottom, they all wonder what's his hurry, but they heap savvy when they see what's following him. He don't slow up none when he reaches camp, so the boys hand him some remarks like, "What's your hurry, Bill, won't you stay to eat?" "Don't hurry, Bill, you got lots of time." "If you're going to Medicine Hat, a little more to the left!"

Bullard's red-eyed by this time, and, of course these remarks cheer him up a whole lot. A little more and Bill would bite himself. If he had a gun, there'd be a massacre. Finally, the hoss wrangler who's afraid Bill will mix with the saddle band, rides out and herds the whole muss into the rope corral.

When Bullard dismounts he don't say nothing an' it don't look safe to ask questions.

Bill's mighty quiet for days. About a week later somebody says something about killin' two birds with one stone. "Yes," says Bill, "maybe you'll kill two birds with one stone but don't ever bet you can get two anythings with one rope."

A Savage Santa Claus

⁶⁶TALKIN' ABOUT Christmas," said Bedrock, as we smoked in his cabin after supper, an' the wind howled as it sometimes can on a blizzardy December night," puts me in mind of one I spent in the '60s. Me 'n a feller named Jake Mason, but better knowed as Beaver, is trappin' an' prospectin' on the head of the Porcupine. We've struck some placer, but she's too cold to work her. The snow's drove all the game out of the country, an' barrin' a few beans and some flour, we're plum out of grub, so we decide we'd better pull our freight before we're snowed in.

"The winter's been pretty open till then, but the day we start there's a storm breaks loose that skins everything I ever seed. It looks like the snow-maker's been holdin' back, an' turned the whole winter supply loose at once. Cold? Well, it would make a polar bear hunt cover.

"About noon it lets up enough so we can see our pack-hosses. We're joggin' along at a good gait, when old Baldy, our lead pack-hoss, stops an' swings 'round in the trail, bringin' the other three to a stand. His whinner causes me to raise my head, an' lookin' under my hat brim, I'm plenty surprised to see an old log shack not ten feet to the side of the trail.

"'I guess we'd better take that cayuse's advice,' says Beaver, pintin' to Baldy, who's got his ears straightened, lookin' at us as much as to say: 'What, am I packin' fer Pilgrims; or don't you know enough to get in out of the weather? It looks like you'd loosen these packs.' So, takin' Baldys hunch, we unsaddle.

"This cabin's mighty ancient. It's been two rooms, but the ridge-pole on the rear one's rotted an' let the roof down. The door's wide open an' hangs on a wooden hinge. The animal smell I get on the inside tells me there ain't no humans lived there for many's the winter. The floor's strewn with pine combs an' a few scattered bones, showin' it's been the home of mountain-rats an' squirrels. Takin' it all 'n all. it ain't no palace, but, in this storm, it looks mighty snug, an' when we get a blaze started in the fireplace an' the beans goin' it's comfortable.

"The door to the back's open, an' by the light of the fire, I can see the roof hangin' down V-shaped, leavin' quite a little space agin the wall. Once I had a notion of walkin' in an' prospectin' the place, but there's somethin' ghostly about it an' I change my mind.

"When we're rollin' in that night, Beaver asks me what day of the month it is.

"'If I'm right on my dates, says I, 'this is the evenin' the kids hang up their socks.'

"'The hell it is,' says he. 'Well, here's one camp Santy'll probably over-look. We ain't got no socks nor no place to hang 'em, an' I don't think the old boy'd savvy our foot-rags.' That's the last I remember till I'm waked up along in the night by somethin' monkeyin' with the kettle.

"If it wasn't fer a snufflin' noise I could hear, I'd a tuk it fer a trade-rat, but with this noise, it's no guess with me, an' I call the turn all right, 'cause when I take a peek, there, humped between me an' the fire is the most robust silvertip I ever see. In size, he resembles a load of hay. The fire's down low, but there's enough light to give me his outline. He's humped over, busy with the beans, snifflin' an' whinin' pleasant, like he enjoys 'em, I nudged Beaver easy, an' whispers: 'Santy Claus is here.'

"He don't need but one look. 'Yes,' says he, reachin' for his Henry, 'but he ain't brought nothin' but trouble, an' more'n a sock full of that. You couldn't crowd it into a wagon-box.'

"This whisperin' disturbs Mr. Bear, an' he straightens up till he near touches the ridge-pole. He looks eight feet tall. Am I scared? Well, I'd tell a

His whinner causes me to raise my head, an' lookin' under my hat, I'm plenty surprised to see an old log shack not ten feet from the side of the trail.

man. By the feelin' runnin' up an' down my back, if I had bristles, I'd resemble a wild hog. The cold sweat's drippin' off my nose, an' I ain't got nothin' on me but sluice-ice.

"The bark of Beaver's Henry brings me out of this scare. The bear goes over, upsettin' a kettle of water, puttin' the fire out. If it wasn't for a stream of fire runnin' from Beaver's weapon, we'd be in plumb darkness. The bear's up agin, bellerin, an' bawlin', and comin' at us mighty warlike, and by the time I get my Sharpe's workin', I'm near choked with smoke. It's the noisiest muss I was ever mixed up in. Between the smoke, the barkin' of the guns an' the bellerin' of the bear, it's like hell on a holiday.

"I'm gropin, for another ca'tridge when I hear the lock on Beaver's gun click, an' I know his magazine's dry. Lowerin' my hot gun, I listen. Everythin's quiet now. In the suddin stillness I can hear the drippin of blood. It's the bear's life runnin' out.

" 'I guess it's all over,' says Beaver, kind of shaky. 'It was a short fight, but a fast one, an' hell was poppin' while she lasted.'

"When we get the fire lit, we take a look at the battle ground. There lays Mr. Bear in a ring of blood, with a hide so full of holes he wouldn't hold hay. I don't think there's a bullet went round him.

"This excitement wakens us so we don't sleep no more that night. We breakfast on bear meat. He's an old bear an' it's pretty stout, but a feller livin' on beans and bannacks straight for a couple of weeks don't kick much on flavor, an' we're at a stage where meat's meat.

"When it comes day, me an' Beaver goes lookin' over the bear's bedroom. You know, daylight drives away ha'nts, an' this room don't look near so ghostly as it did last night. After winnin' this fight, we're both mighty brave. The

This whisperin' disturbs Mr. Bear an' he straightens up till he near touches the ridge pole.

roof caved in with four or five feet of snow on, makes the rear room still dark, so, lightin' a pitch-pine glow, we start explorin'.

The bark of Beaver's Henry brings me out of this scare.

"The first thing we bump into is the bear's bunk. There's a rusty pick layin' up against the wall, an' a gold-pan on the floor, showin' us that the human that lived there was a miner. On the other side of the shack we ran onto a pole bunk, with a weather-wrinkled buffalo robe an' some rotten blankets. The way the roof slants, we can't see into the bed, but by usin' an axe an' choppin' the legs off, we lower it to view. When Beaver raises the light, there's the framework of a man. He's layin' on his left side, like he's sleepin', an' looks like he cashed in easy. Across the bunk, under his head, is an old-fashioned cap-'n-ball rifle. On the bedpost hangs a powder horn an' pouch, with a belt, an' skinnin' knife. These things tell us that this man's a pretty old-timer.

"Findin' the pick an' gold-pan causes us to look more careful for what he'd been diggin'. We explore the bunk from top to bottom, but nary a find. All day long we prospects. That evenin', when we're fillin' up on bear meat, beans and bannacks, Beaver says he's goin' to go through the bear's bunk; so, after we smoke, relightin' our torches, we start our search again.

"Sizin' up the bear's nest, we see he'd laid there quite a while. It looks like Mr. Silvertip, when the weather gets cold, starts huntin' a winter location for his long snooze. Runnin' onto this cabin, vacant, and lookin' like it's for rent, he jumps the claim an' would have been snoozin' there yet, but our fire warmin' up the place, fools him. He thinks it's spring an' steps out to look at the weather. On the way he strikes this breakfast of beans, an' they hold him till we object.

"We're lookin' over this nest when somethin' catches my eye on the edge of the waller. It's a hole, roofed over with willers.

" 'Well, I'll be damned. There's his cache,' says Beaver, who's eyes has follered mine. It don't take a minute to kick these willers loose, an' there lays a buckskin sack with five hundred dollars in dust in it.

" 'Old Santy Claus, out there,' says Beaver, pointin' to the bear through the door, 'didn't load our socks, but he brought plenty of meat an' showed us the cache, for we'd never a-found it if he hadn't raised the lid.'

"The day after Christmas we buried the bones, wrapped in one of our blankets, where we'd found the cache. It was the best we could do.

" 'I guess the dust's ours,' says Beaver. 'There's no papers to show who's his kin-folks,' so we splits the pile an' leaves him sleepin' in the tomb he built for himself."

Bab's Skees

66OLD BABCOCK," says Rawhide, "could tell yarns that's scary. We're talking about skees when Bab springs this one.

" 'Me and Gumboot Williams are camped on Swimmin' Women," says Bab. "We was set afoot by the Crows. It's back in seventy-six—we'd saved our hair and we're hidin'. The snow comes early that fall—we're away up on the Swimmin' Women. There's lots of game, but we're huggin' camp close—

we're afraid of war parties, but a little later when we know Injuns have quit prowlin', we get bold. We're right comfortable, but we're running low on meat.

" 'It's hard travelin'—the snow's so deep.I don't know nothin' about makin' snowshoes so I decide it's easier to build skees and hew out a pair of lodge pole pine. I try 'em out around camp. I can't make much time, but I keep on top of the snow. It's hard climbing till I wrap them with a strip of buffalo robe, makin' a kind of rough lock. So, one morning, I starts climbing the south side of the Snowies. I'm keepin' to the open country, avoidin' timber. 'Tain't long till I jump five blacktail but don't get a shot.

" 'About noon, I'm pretty high and stop to get my wind while I'm viewing the country. It's so clear I can see the Musselshell way south. Suddenly I see about two miles below me, a band of about twenty elk—some of them is laying down. I'm packing a forty-four Henry, so after throwing a shell in the barrel, I slip my rough locks and start, an' it ain't a minute till I know I've lost control. I'm riding a cyclone with the bridle off or somebody's kicked the lid off and I'm coming like a bat out of hell. I can smell the smoke of my skees, they're sure warming up when I hit astride of a dead lodgepole. It looks like this would stop me, but don't ever think it. She busts at the root, bends over and when I shoot off the end, she's trimmed as slick as a fish-pole—there ain't a limb on her. I must have split about fifty of these when these elk hear the noise. They're leaving their beds when I come hurling off the end of a lodge pole and light straddle of the biggest bull there. I stay with him till he wipes me off with his horns. I land this time sittin' on my skees. I've still got my Henry and I'm fightin' mad. While I'm passin' this bunch they look like their backing up. I throw down a big cow and break her shoulders. I'm still traveling south but ain't got time to skin my killin'. After trimming several hundred more acres of lodge poles, the country levels and I slow down and finally quit. From my belt down, I'm dressed like a savage, but I'm warm both ways from the middle, I'm plumb feverish. I'm still wearing a belt and lucky I've got my rough locks. It's easy back tracking—of course, there are long distances there ain't no tracks, but while I'm in the air I'm cutting swaths in the timber that looks like a landslide. When I get to the cow, I take the tongue and loins. I don't reach camp till dark.

" 'I think,' says Bab, shaking out his pipe, 'that Injun webs is the best if you ain't in a hurry.' "

Cowboy loses

Fashions

IN GRAND DAD'S time when a man starts looking for his mate he's sure gambling. If the lady limps he might think her shoes hurt, but maybe she's got a wooden leg, with the yards of garments she's wearing, he can't tell. What she's got on would overdress a ball room today. He's only got two safe bets—her face and her hands. Of course she's wearing long hair, but her head is another gamble; maybe it's got bumps like a summer squash; and maybe the hair that hides it is a wig. She'd look the same with a night-cap on in a feather bed. As I said before "—our Grand Paws was sure gamblers!"

It's different today. Bobbed hair, short skirts, low front and back—every rag she's wearing wouldn't pad a crutch. If you think you're getting the worst

Our Grand Paws was sure gamblers.

of it, take the lady to the seashore, get her wet in her one-piece suit and you don't need no X-ray—the cards are face up on the table; scars, warts or pimples, they are all in sight—all you got to do now is find out what brand of cigarettes she uses.

I used to think that men could stand more punishment than women, but I was wrong. In winter a girl wears a fox skin, but her brisket is bared to the weather, and their aint nothin' on her that's warmer than a straw hat, but she don't pound her feet nor swing her arms. If she's cold nobody knows it. If a man would go out dressed this way, there aint doctors enough in the world to save him. No sir, a woman can go farther with a lipstick than a man can with a Winchester and a side of bacon.

Maybe these hump-backs knows where they's goin' but the driver ain't got no idea, ·* *   but judgin' from the sun he's goin' south.

Broke Buffalo

"THERE USED to be a man on the Yellerstone," says Rawhide, "that catches a pair of yearling buffalo. He handles them hump-back cows till they're plumb gentle—they hang around the ranch like any other cows.

"One day he decides to put them in the yoke. That bump fits back of the yoke and in all ways they are built for work. But he finds looks are deceivin' when he rigs a pole on a pair of old hind wheels, making a kind of cart—it's no sulky, tain't built for speed, but that's what it's used for. They ain't hard to yoke. He's whacked bulls and skinned mules but when he gets up behind this team, he can't find no team talk the pair savvies. He's usin' rope reins but they might as well be thread—he couldn't bend their neck with a canthook.

"Finally, they start. Maybe these hump-backs know where they's going, but this driver ain't got no idea. Tain't long till he's in a country he ain't never

He's got his plow sunk to the beam. * * * They started north an' that's where they're goin'.

saw, but judgin' from the sun, he's going south an' both wheels are smoking. They run over a jackrabbit and pass a band of antelope that's doing their damdest. It's afternoon when the hurry-up party hits a rut that breaks the driver's hold and he lands in a patch of buck brush. He's dam glad of it—he's plumb tired holdin'. He don't know how far they went but don't get home till noon next day. About a week later his team shows up at the corral—they're still packing the yoke. They don't show no signs of being jaded.

"Next spring a neighbor talks him into breaking sod with them. He gets to thinkin' this over and knowin' they got the power, he hooks them onto a plow. This time he heads them north, but this direction suits them. It's springtime and they don't mind going north. He's got his plow sunk to the beam— it slows their gait some but he can't turn them. They started north and that's where they's going. Streams don't stop them and when he quits the handles, they's still plowing north.

"He finds out that these animals travel north in the spring and south in the fall. If he could find a country with seasons no longer than this field, they'd do good for a driving team. If he was fixed so he could spend his winters in Mexico and his summers in Canada, they'd just be the thing. He hears from them through a friend late that summer—they're north of the Teton plowing south."

Suddenly something happens. Lepley can't tell whether it's an earthquake or a cyclone, but everything' went from under him an' he's sailin' off, but he's flying low an' using his face for a rough lock.

Lepley's Bear

"OLD MAN LEPLEY tells me one time about a bear he was near enough
to shake hands with but they don't get acquainted. He's been living
on hog side till he's near starved. So, one day he saddled up and starts
prowling for something fresh. There's lots of black tail in the country but
they have been hunted till they are shy, so after riding a while without seeing
nothing he thinks he'll have better luck afoot. So, the first park he hits, he
stakes his hoss. It's an old beaver meadow with bluejoint to his cayuse's
knees, and about the center (like it's put there for him) is a dead cottonwood
snag handy to stake his hoss to.

"After leaving the park he ain't gone a quarter of a mile till he notices
the taller branches of a chokecherry bush movin'. There's no wind and Lepley
knows that bush don't move without something pushing it, so naturally he's
curious. Tain't long till he heap savvys. It's a big silvertip and he's sure
busy berrying. There's lots of meat here and bear grease is better than any
boughten lard. So, Lepley pulls down on him, aimin' for his heart. Mr. Bear
bites where the ball hits. It makes old silver damn disagreeable—he starts
bawlin' and comin'.

"As I said before, there ain't no wind. It's the smoke from his gun hovering
over Lepley that tips it off where he's hiding. He's packing a Sharps carbine
an' he ain't got time to reload, so he turns this bear hunt into a foot race. It's
a good one, but it looks like the man'll take second money. When he reaches
the park his hoss has grazed to the near end. Lepley don't stop to bridle, but
leaps for the saddle.

"About this time the hoss sees what's hurrying the rider. One look's enough.
In two jumps, he's giving the best hes' got. Suddenly something happens.
Lepley can't tell whether it's an earthquake or a cyclone but everything went
from under him, and he's sailin' off but he's flying low and uses his face for a
rough lock, and stops agin some bushes. When he wakes up he don't hear harps
nor smell smoke. It ain't till then he remembers he don't untie his rope. The
snag snapped off, and his hoss is tryin' to drag it out of the country, and Mr.
Bear, by the sound of breaking brush, is hunting a new range, and it won't be
anywhere near where they met. When his hoss stops on the end of the rope,
that old snag snaps and all her branches scatter over the park. I guess Mr.
Bear thinks the hoss has turned on him. Maybe some of them big limbs bounced
on him and he thinks the hoss has friends and they're throwing clubs at him.
Anyhow, Mr. Bear gives the fight to Lepley and the hoss.

"Lepley says that for months he has to walk that old hoss a hundred yards
before he can spur him into a lope and you could stake him on a hairpin and
he'd stay.

Dog Eater

66 "A MAN THAT ain't never been hungry can't tell nobody what's good to eat." says Rawhide. "I eat raw sow bosom and frozen biscuit when it tasted like a Christmas dinner.

"Bill Gurd tells me he's caught one time. He's been ridin' since daybreak and ain't had a bite. It's plum dark when he hits a breed's camp. This old breed shakes hands and tells Bill he's welcome, so after strippin' his saddle and hobblin' his hoss, he steps into the shack. Being wolf hungry, he notices the old woman's cooking bannacks at the mud fire. Tired and hungry like Bill

Friendship goes yelpin' into the woods an' I'm standin' like a kid with his tail in my hand.

is, the warmth and the smell of grub makes this cottonwood shack that ain't much more than a windbreak, look like a palace.

" 'Tain't long till the old woman hands him a tin plate loaded with stew and bannacks with hot tea for a chaser. He don't know what kind of meat it is but he's too much of a gentleman to ask. So he don't look a gift hoss in the mouth. After he fills up, while he's smokin' the old man spreads down some blankets and Bill beds down.

"Next mornin' he gets the same for breakfast. Not being so hungry, he's more curious, but don't ask no questions. On the way out to catch hiss hoss he gets an answer. A little ways from the cabin, he passes a fresh dog hide pegged down on the ground. It's like seeing the hole card—it's no gamble what that stew was made of, but it was good and Bill held it.

"I knowed another fellow one time that was called 'Dog Eatin' ' Jack. I never knowed how he got his name that's hung to him, till I camp with him. This old boy is a prospector and goes gopherin' round the hills, hopin' he'll find something.

"I'm huntin' hosses one spring and ain't found nothing but tracks. I'm up on the Lodgepole in the foothills; it's sundown and my hoss has went lame. We're limping along slow when I sight a couple of hobbled cayuses in a beaver meadow. One of these hosses is wearing a Diamond G iron, the other a quarter circle block hoss. They're both old cow ponies. I soon locate their owner's camp—it's a lean-to in the edge of the timber.

"While I'm lookin' over the layout, here comes the owner. It's the Dog Eater. After we shake hands I unsaddle and stake out my tired hoss. When we're filled up on the best he's got, (which is beans, bacon and frying pan bread, which is good filling for hungry men), we're sittin' smokin' and its then I ask him if he ever lived with Injuns.

" 'You're thinkin'!' says he, 'about my name. It does sound like Injun, but they don't hang it on me. It happens about ten winters ago. I'm way back in the diamond range; I've throwed my hosses about ten mile out in the foothills where's there good feed and less snow. I build a lean-to, a good one, and me and my dog settles down. There's some beaver here and I got out a line of traps and figger on winterin' here. Ain't got much grub but there's lots of game in the hills and my old needle gun will get what the traps won't.

" 'Snow comes early an dlots of it. About three days after the storm I step on a loose boulder and sprain my ankle. This puts me plumb out; I can't more than keep my fire alive. All the time I'm running short of grub. I eat a couple of skinned beaver, I'd throwed away one day. My old dog brings in a snowshoe rabbit to camp and maybe you don't think he's welcome. I cut in two with him but, manlike, I give him the front end. That's the last we got.

" 'Old Friendship (that's the dog's name) goes out every day but he don't get nothing and I know he ain't cheating—he's too holler in the flanks. After about four days of living on thoughts, Friendship starts watchin' like he's afraid. He thinks maybe I'll put him in the pot, but he sizes me up wrong. If I'd do that, I hope I choke to death.

" 'The sixth day I'm sizin' him up. He's laying near the fire. He's a hound with a long meaty tail. Says I to myself, 'Oxtail soup! What's the matter with dog tail? He don't use it for nothing but sign talk but it's like cutting the hands off a dummy. But the eighth day, with hunger and pain in my ankle, I plumb locoed and I can't get that dog's tail out of my mind. So, a little before noon, I slip up on him while he's sleeping, with the ax. In a second it's all over.

Friendship goes yelpin' into the woods and I am sobbin' like a kid, with his tail in my hand.

" 'The water is already boiling in the pot an' as soon as I singe the hair off it's in the pot. I turned a couple of flour sacks inside out and dropped them in and there's enough flour to thicken the soup. It's about dark. I fill up and if it weren't for thinkin', it would have been good. I could have eat it all but I held out over half for Friendship, in case he come back.

" 'It must be midnight when he pushes into the blankets with me. I take him in my arms. He's as cold as a dead snake, and while I'm holdin' him tight, I'm crying like a baby. After he warms up a little, I get up and throw some wood on the fire and call Friendship to the pot. He eats every bit of it. He don't seem to recognize it. If he does, being a dog, he forgives.

" 'We go back to the blankets. It's just breaking day when he slides out, whinin' and sniffin' the air with his ears cocked and his bloody stub wobblin'. I look the way he's pointin' and not twenty-five yards from the lean-to stands a big elk. There's a fine snow fallin'; the wind's right for us. I ain't a second gettin' my old needle gun but I'm playin' safe—I'm coming Injun on him. I use my ram rod for a rest. When old needle speaks, the bull turns over—his neck's broken. Tain't long till we both get to that bull and we're both eatin' raw, warm liver. I've seen Injuns do this but I never thought I was that much wolf, but it was sure good that morning.

" 'He's a big seven-point bull—old and pretty tough, but me and Friendship was looking for quantity, not quality and we got it. That meat lasted till we got out.'

" 'What became of Friendship?' says I.

" 'He died two years ago,' says Jack. 'But he died fat.' "

That reminds me

A Gift Horse

CHARLEY FURIMAN tells me about a hoss he owns and if you're able to stay on him he'll take you to the end of the trail. The gent Charley got him from, says he, "Gentle?" He's a pet." (This man hates to part with him). "He's a lady's hoss. You can catch him anywhere with a biscuit."

Next day Charley finds out he's a lady's hoss, all right, but he don't like men. Furiman ain't a mile from his corral when he slips the pack. Charley crawls him again kinder careful and rides him sixty miles an' he don't turn a hair. Next day he saddles him he acts like he's harmless but he's looking for

I don't miss none of them boulders and where I light there's nothin' gives but different parts of me.

something. He's out about ten mile. Charley notices he travels with one ear down. This ain't a good sign, but Charley gets careless and about noon he comes to a dry creek bed where there's lots of boulders. That's what this cayuse is looking for 'cause right in the middle of this boulder strewn flat is where he breaks in two and unloads. Charley tells me, "I don't miss none of them boulders an' where I light there's nothing gives but different parts of me. For a while I wonder where I'm at and when things do clear up it comes to me right quick. I forgot to bring the biscuits. How am I going to catch him? If I had a Winchester, I'd catch him just over the eye.

"To make a long story short, I followed him back to the ranch afoot. Walking ain't my strong holt an' these boulder bumps don't help me none. Next morning after a good night's sleep, I feel better. Going out to the corral, I offer this cayuse a biscuit, thinkin' I'll start off friendly. He strikes at me and knocks my hat off. My pardner tries to square it by telling me I ain't got the right kind. 'That's a lady's hoss,' says he, 'and being a pet, he wants them little lady's biscuits, its enough to make him sore, handing him them sour doughs.'

"While I'm getting my hat, I happen to think of a friend of mine that's got married and I ain't give him no wedding present. This friend of mine is a bronk rider named Con Price. So while my heart's good, I saddle a gentle hoss and lead this man-hater over and presents him to Price with my best wishes.

"I don't meet Con till next fall on the beef roundup. He ain't too friendly. Next morning when we're roping hosses, he steps up to me and says, kinder low, holdin' out his hand to shake, 'Charley, I'm letting bygones be bygones, but if I get married again anywhere in your neighborhood, don't give me no wedding presents. If you do you'll get lots of flowers.'"

Rawhide Rawlins

Ranches

⁶⁶"THE COW RANCHES that I knowed," says Rawhide, " is nothing like
them they're running today. In the old days, it wasn't much, only a place
to winter. They were on a stream or river bottom. The buildings were
made of what the country gave—logs, either cottonwood or pine in the north.
They had one house—maybe two, with a shed between, a stable and a pole corral.
All these buildings were dirt roof, some had no floor but ground. There was
no fences, not even a pasture. South of Colorado these buildings were adobe.
Out on the treeless plains where there's no timely, they were sod.

"A few tons of wild hay were put up for a little bunch of saddle hosses
for winter. This was put up, not by cowpunchers but by some outsider that
wanted work.

"Cows sound like milk but if a cowpuncher got milk it was Eagle Brand.
Cowpunchers might work a brand over or steal a slick ear but he wouldn't steal
milk from a calf.

"I never knowed but one woman on a cow ranch and she wore moccasins
an' smoked willow bark. I'm talkin' about the days of the open range when
there wasn't a wire from the Arctic Sea to the Gulf of Mexico. There were no
dogs, no chickens—some had a cat, but he had to rustle for his grub during the
summer months. There was a cat hole in the door with a little swinging door
that the cat could open, and don't think he couldn't handle it—'specially if a
coyote, or his big cousin, Mr. Bob Cat showed up. He liked to see the snow
come 'cause he knowed that would drive the punchers home and maybe you
think he didn't purr when the boys came home; he was sure loving.

"Barring line riders that were stationed at a lonesome line camp, cowpunchers put in their time at the stage station playing monty or stud poker.
Most cow hands were whisky drinkers. Some of them wintered in cow towns.
either tending bar, gambling or working in a livery stable—he could hold down
any of these jobs. The booze joints he worked in, he tended bar with his hat
on. He was good around hosses, and most always was a gambler. On the
range, he played on a blanket, in town, he could generally hold his own on a
round table agin tin horns. Some punchers hung around at the ranch making
hackamores and ropes. Reading matter was scarce—a saddle catalog, maybe
a back number Police Gazette, sometimes a well-worn stray novel. In the long
winter nights their light was coal oil lamps or candles—sometimes they were
forced to use a bitch which was a tin cup filled with bacon grease and a twisted
rag wick. It didn't only give light—it gave its owners a smell like a New
England dinner.

"When spring came cowpunchers gathered hosses, an' rode bog till the
roundup time.

"Most of the cow ranches I've seen lately was like a big farm. A bungalow
with all modern improvements, a big red barn that holds white faced bulls an'
hornless milk cows. The corrals are full of fancy chickens, there's a big garage

filled with all kinds of cars, and at the bunkhouse that sets back where the owner and his family can't see or hear them, are the hands.

"You might see a man with a big hat, boots and spurs—he's the fence rider—but most of them wear bib overalls. The boss wears puttees and a golf cap.

"The bungalow, that's got electric lights an' hot and cold water. There's a piana that you play with your feet and a radio, a Mah Jong set and a phonograph.

Most of the cow ranches I've seen lately was like a big farm. A bungalow with all modern improvements, an' big red barn that holds white face bulls. The boss wears puttees an' a golf cap.

In the old days the cow ranch wasn't much only a place to winter. They had one house—maybe two, with a shed between.

The owner, if he's an old timer, don't care for this. He'd rather camp in the bunkhouse and talk to some old bow leg about cows that wore horns. But maybe the woman he's tied to is the new kind. If she is, she's got pa whip-broke. She's out for sheriff. She's that kind. She's been wearin' the bell since she stepped in her loop, so pa, like any other good pack-hoss, takes anything you put on him. He's wearin' golf socks and knickerbockers and when he meets his old friends, looks ashamed.

"If they've got a son or daughter, they come home during vacation. The daughter goes to finishin' school, she's got her hair bobbed. At this school she learns to smoke and wears less clothes and makes 'em stay on with no visible support than any since the days of Eve. If she or her brother ride at all, they ride with an English saddle an' English boots. Both her and her brother can knock a golf ball so far a blood hound couldn't find it in a week—but there's a hired girl in the house to pass the biscuits.

"Son can play football. He's good with the gloves and can do all kinds of tricks with Injun clubs, but with an ax he's plumb harmless. He couldn't split enough wood to cook a flapjack in a month. He can find the button that turns on the light but he couldn't find one of his dad's calves in a corral, with a bell on. Maybe he could find work, but he never looks for it.

"All these folks have been across the big water. Paw didn't care to go, but ma was wearing the bell, so he trails along—him an' his checkbook. They've traveled in the Alps with a Swiss guide but nary one of them ever saw the Yellerstone or Glacier park.

"The cow ranch today," says Rawhide, "is a place to make money to go somewheres else."

Now-a-days it's white face bulls an' hornless milk cows.

Range Horses

"RANGE HOSSES," says Rawhide, "don't ask nothing of men. Since Cortez brought them they've been taking care of themselves. They've been a long time learning—from the land of drought to the country of deep snows and long winters, they ranged.

"The Injun used to tame wolves to move their camps till the Spaniard came. These dogs being meat eaters it kept the red men busy feeding his folks and his dogs. It's a cinch that lots of the time the whole outfit went hungry. Im guessing that in those days that nobody knows about the red men followed the wolf and when able, drove him from his kill, and the wolf had the best end of it. But with a hoss under him it was different. The wolf followed the red man and got part of his kill. Some Injuns call the hoss the big dog but I'm telling about hosses.

"All other animals cached their young when they went to water. When a colt was born, his mother never left him, and in a short time, he would travel

In fly time they bunch up and stand head and tail each hoss usin' the tail of pardner as a fly brush.

with his maw. Wolves don't have much chance. Hosses stay in bands—if a wolf or wolves show up, they won't run like other animals, they bunch; and range hosses are dangerous at both ends, striking and kicking. A wolf likes something easy. After he feels the hoofs of a range mare a few times, he quits—it takes his appetite.

"When winter comes, range hosses don't hug the brush like cows and starve to death—they hunt the ridges where the snow blows off. When he gets cold, the whole band will run and warm up—if the snow's deep, he paws to the grass. This keeps him warm. Nature gives him a winter coat. Sometimes, when his belly's full, he'll hunt a wind-break. Sometimes a lion will get a colt, but not often. Range hosses like open country and won't stay in the brush only long enough to water.

"Hosses love pure cold water. In running water, which they like best, most of them drink with their heads up stream, every hoss trying to get up stream above the rile. I've seen bands of hosses at a prairie spring waiting their turn to drink where it was cold and clear. As I said before, hosses like good water, but in countries where water ain't good, they drink anything that's wet. In fly time they bunch and stand heads and tails, each hoss using the tail of pardner as a fly brush. If there's a breeze they hunt high ground; if it's still, they pick bare ground where there's lots of dust. In saddle bands, like you'll see on roundups, hosses will stay in groups from two to four or five.

"Some hosses will stay friends for years; others, like men, are changeable. A band of hosses turn their hind quarters to a rain or snow storm. They will, if driven, face a storm but it's hard to make them go sideways. Range hosses in a hilly country stand with their heads down hill. You could drive a band of hosses up the steepest kind of a hill but nobody that I ever knowed could drive a bunch straight down (that goes with cows, too)—they'd sidle it every time.

"Hosses raised on the plains don't like the mountains and if there's any chance they pull out. A hoss loves the range where he was foaled and will drift hundreds of miles to get back. If you're traveling with strange hosses and camp as long as they are tired and hungry, they stay, but if there's a bunch quitter, watch him when he fills up—he'll drift and travel.

"Most hosses are good swimmers but few of them like it. If you want to play safe swimming a hoss, loosen your cinches and jerk your bridle off. Maybe you won't come out just where you wanted, but you'll come out. Many a man has drowned himself and hoss by pulling his hoss over. If you're lost in a blizzard, give your cayuse his head—he'll take you to shelter—it's hard to lose an animal.

"In the dark, don't spur a hoss where he don't want to go. There's lots of times a hoss knows more than a man. A man that says a hoss don't know nothin' don't know much about hosses."

Dunc McDonald

"DUNC MC DONALD tells about a buffalo hunt he has when he's a kid," says Rawhide. "Like all things that happen that's worth while, it's a long time ago. He's traveling with his people—they're making for the buffalo country. They're across the range—they ain't seen much—an old bull once in a while that ain't worth shootin' at, so they don't disturb nothin'. They're lookin' for cow meat and lots of it.

"Dunc's traveling ahead of the women with the men. As I said, it's a long time ago when Injuns ain't got many guns—they're mostly armed with bows and arrows. There's one old man packing a rifle. It's a Hudson Bay flint-

Dunc sees a few buffalo in some broken hills, an' tells this old man, if he'll lend him his gun, he'll get meat.

lock but a good gun, them days. Duncan is young and has good eyes that go with youth. He sees a few buffalo in some broken hills, and tells this old man if he'll lend him his gun, he'll get meat. The old man don't say nothin', but taking the gun from its skin cover, hands it to Dunc. Dunc wants bullets and the powder horn but the old man signs that the gun is loaded and one ball is enough for any good hunter. The wolf hunts with what teeth he's got.

"Dunc knows he won't get no more so he rides off. There ain't much wind, but Dunc's gettin' what there is, and keepin' behind some rock croppin's he gets pretty close. There are five cows, all laying down. Pretty soon he quits his pony and crawls to within twenty-five yard and pulls down a fat cow. When his gun roars, they all jump and run but the cow he shoots don't make three jumps till she's down.

"When Dunc walks up she's laying on her belly with her feet under her.

"There's only one hold," says Dunc, "shorter than a tail hold on a buffalo—that of a bear."

She's small but fat. When Dunc puts his foot agin her to push her over, she gets up and is red-eyed. She sure shows war. The only hold Dunc can see is her tail and he ain't slow takin' it. The tail hold on a buffalo is mighty short, but he's clamped on. She's tryin' to turn but he's keepin' her steered right—and he's doing fine till she starts kickin'. The first one don't miss his ear the width of a hair. If you never saw a buffalo kick it's hard to tell you what they can do, but Dunc ain't slow slippin' his hold.

"There's nothin' left but to run for it. This rock croppin's ain't over two feet high, but it's all there is. These rocks are covered with ground cedar and Dunc dives into this. He gophers down in this cedar till a hawk couldn't find him. He lays there a long time, his heart poundin' his ribs like it will break through. When the scare works out of him he raises and there agin the rock rim lays the cow—it's a lung shot and she's bled to death.

" 'There's only one hold,' says Dunc, 'shorter than a tail hold on a buffalo —that of a bear.' "

She sure shows war.

Safety First! But Where Is It?

"SAFETY FIRST is the big holler today," says Rawhide, "but how do you know when and where you're safe? These days its hard to find. A rocking chair looks gentle but when an earthquake comes along its no safer nor as safe as a locoed bronk. A bronk might get you in the clear. I never heard of a salmon from fresh water hurting anybody, but out of a can he's often dangerous.

"One time I'm on a coach," says Rawhide. "I'm sitting up with the driver. We're going down a steep grade when the brake pole snaps. The coach starts crowding the wheelers. Playing safe, I jumps. I roll down a bank about forty feet an' stop in a bed of cactus. This driver's a good one and starts

This driver's a good one, an' starts playin' the silk on the six, an' keeps them ahead of the wheels.

playing the silk on his six, and keeps them ahead of the wheels. They don't run twenty-five yards till the man with the ribbons finds an up-grade, straightens his team and stops. The coach is loaded and nobody gets a scratch. But me! That's playing safe. I look like a porcupine and it takes weeks to pluck me.

"Old Bedrock Jim tells me one time about him and his pardner. They're prospecting in the Big Horns. One morning they're out of meat. They ain't gone far till they jump an elk. It's a bull. Bedrock gets the first shot—that's all he needs. The bull goes to his knees and rolls over. They both walk up laying their guns agin a log. The bull's laying with his head under him. Bedrock notices the blood on the bull's neck and thinks his neck's broke, but when he grabs a horn and starts to straighten him out to stick him, the bull gets up and he ain't friendly and goes to war with Bedrock and his pardner. He's between the hunters and their guns. There's nothing to do but give the bull the fight.

"Bedrock makes a scrub pine that's agin a rock ledge. This tree won't hold two, so his pardner finds a hole under the ledge. It's late in the winter; there's plenty of snow and the wind's in the north. There ain't much comfort up this jack pine. When Bedrock looks around, he notices that Jack Williams (that's his pardner's name), keeps coming out of the hole. Then the bull will charge them. Jack goes back but he don't stay long. The bull ain't only creased and he's mighty nasty. His hair's all turned the wrong way and the way he rattles his horns agin the rocks around that hole tells he ain't jokin', But Bedrock can't savvy why when the bull steps back, Jack comes out of the hole.

"Bedrock's getting cold and plumb out of patience and he finally hollers down from his perch, 'If you'd stay in that hole, you damn fool, that bull would leave and give us a chance to get away.' Jack is taking his turn outside. The bull charges. Jack ducks in as the bull scrapes his horns on the rocks. The bull backs away, shakin' his head. This time when he shows, he yells up to Bedrock, 'Stay in the hole, hell! There's a bear in the hole.'

"It's near dark when they get away. Bedrock gets on a lower limb and flags the bull with his coat. He's taking a long chance. The footing he's got, if he ever slips, it's good-bye. As I said before, the bull ain't joshing but he holds the bull till Jack gets his gun, and when he does he sure kills him. He empties his Henry into him and not a ball goes by."

Jack goes back, but he don't stay long. The bull's only creased an' he's mighty nasty.

The Trail of the Reel Foot

"I'M GETTIN' MIGHTY weary of holin' up in this line camp," said Long Wilson, scratching the frost from the window and gazing discontentedly out at the storm. "If the snow ever lets up, it'll be fine trackin' weather, 'n' chances 'll be good for a blacktail over on Painted Ridge."

"Tracks 'd do you a whole lot of good, old scout," said Bowlegs, sitting up cross-legged in the bunk and rolling a cigarette. "You couldn't track a bed-wagon through a boghole. I ain't forgot last winter, when you're lost on Dog Creek. You're ridin' in a circle, follerin' your own trail, 'n' you'd 'a' been there yet if the Cross H boys hadn't found you. You're a tracker, I don't think."

"Speakin' of trackin'," broke in Dad Lane, the wolfer, "reminds me of a cripple I knowed who goes by the name of Reel Foot. He's one of nature's mistakes, a born deformity. It looks like when Old Lady Nature built him, she starts from the top 'n' does good work till she gets to his middle, 'n' then throws off the job to somebody that's workin' for fun.

"This cripple was before your time, but he's well known on the lower Yellerstone in the early '70s. The first winter I ever see Reel Foot I'm sittin' in a poker game with him. Now, lookin' at him across the table, he'll average up with any man for shape 'n' looks, but at this time, I ain't acquainted with him from his waist down.

"For two weeks I've been eatin' plenty booze, 'n' I'm at that stage where I see things that ain't there. Old Four-Ace Jack that's handin' us the beverage, looks like twins; my sight's doublin' up on me. The game's goin' along smooth enough till I reach for a pot on a pair of aces, 'n' Reel Foot claims I only got one. There's quite a little argument, 'n' while he's convincin' me I spill some chips. When I'm gropin' 'round for 'em under the table, I run onto them hoofs, warped 'n' twisted. As I said before, I ain't acqainted with his hind quarters, 'n' it rattles me till I see feet enough for four men, 'n' there's only two of us playin'. This ends the game with me, so cashin' in, I tell Four-Ace to pour my drink back in the bottle. I'm that shaky I couldn't empty it into a barrel with the head out, 'n' don't swallow no more booze that trip.

"The scare wears off when I get acquainted with Reel Foot, but I never do look at him without wonderin' which way he's goin' to start off. His right foot's straight ahead, natural; the left, p'intin' back on his trail. It's an old sayin', 'a fool for luck,' 'n' in this case, I guess it goes with cripples, for it's these twisted hin' legs of his'n that saves his hide 'n' hair for him once.

"It happens when he first hits the country from Nebrasky. He's camped on the Porcupine, 'n' as trappin's good 'n' he's figurin' on staying awhile, he's throwed up a lean-to of brush. He's one of these kind that don't get lonesome, 'n' 'lows if you don't mix with no worse company than animals you're all right. Livin' so long with cayuses, he savvies 'em 'n' they understand him. They even seem to know what he's talkin' to 'em about.

"One mornin' Reel Foot leaves camp to visit his traps. He's on his pony,

but about a mile down the creek, the brush bein' thick, he quits the cayuse 'n'
goes afoot. After visitin' his traps Reel Foot circles 'round 'n' doubles back on
his old trail a couple of hundred yards below where his hoss is tied. When he
reaches his cayuse he climbs on 'n' rides into camp.

"Now, there's a bunch of Ogallaly Sioux in this country, led by Blood
Lance. They're runnin' buffalo, 'n' one day they find where some whites has
made a killin' 'n' tuk nothin' but the tongues. This waste of meat makes their
hearts bad, 'n' it wouldn't be healthy for no whites they run across. Their
feelin's are stirred up this way when they strike Reel Foot's tracks, which

After studyin' the tracks awhile, they decide the old man's right. They's two one legged
men travelin' in opposite direction.

causes them to pull up their ponies, 'n' every Injun skins his gun. There's
snow on the ground, so the readin's plain. He's wearin' moccasins, but that
don't fool 'em none; they see where he's shuk out his pipe while hes walkin'.
This tells 'em he's a white man, 'cause Injuns don't smoke while they're

travelin' Whenever a redskin lights his pipe, you can bet he's down on his hunkers, takin' comfort.

" 'My brothers,' says one wise old buck who's been sittin' wrapped in his blanket, sayin' nothin', 'are the Ogallalys like the bat that cannot see in the light of the sun? Shall we sit 'n' talk with women while these men with hair on their faces, who leave our meat to rot on the prairie, walk from under our knives 'n' laugh at us? I am old 'n' do not boast of the eye of the hawk, but it's as plain as the travoy tracks in the snow; there are two men.'

"After studyin' the tracks awhile they decide the old man's right. There are two one-legged men travelin' in opposite directions. From the length of the strides showed by the tracks, they figger these men are long in the leg, 'n' must be very tall. They talk it over 'n' decide to split the party 'n' take both trails.

"Of course, they go lookin' for the track of a crutch or wooden leg, but finally the only way they can figger it out is that these two men's travelin' by hoppin', 'n' the tricks these cripples does has them savages guessin'. There's one place where Reel Foot's jumped off a cutbank; it's anyway ten feet straight down. Now for the cripple that jumps down, it is easy, but what's worryin' these Injuns is how the other one-legged man stands flat-footed 'n' bounds up the bank, lightin' easy with no sign of scramblin'.

"When the party that takes the trail towards camp gets to where Reel Foot doubles back, they're plenty puzzled. Injun-like, these fellers are superstitious, 'n' when the tracks run together, they're gettin' scary.

" 'It looks like the tracks of two two-legged men walkin' in opposite directions,' says a young buck named Weasel. 'Or else the one-legged men have found their lost legs.'

"But the old wise man says: 'again the young buck has the eyes of the bat. There are four tracks; two of the right foot 'n' two of the left. These are the tracks of four one-legged men.'

"Some think it's the work of ghosts 'n' are willin' to turn back, but their curiosity downs their fear, 'n' they foller the trail mighty shaky till they run onto where Reel Foot mounts his hoss. Here they figger that two of these one-legged men got off the hoss, while the other two, comin' the opposite way, get on 'n' ride into the willers.

"By this time these savages are so rattled that the snappin' of a twig would turn the whole band back. They're beginnin' to think they've struck the land of one-legged men, 'n' they're follerin' the trail mighty cautious when they sight the smoke of Reel Foot's camp.

"Now when the Reel Foot gets in from his traps, he's mighty leg-weary after draggin' them warped feet of his'n through the snow. So the minute he gets some grub under his belt, he freshens the fire 'n' beds down with his feet stickin' out towards the warmth. He's layin' this way asleep, when these killers come up on him. The minute they sight his feet, every buck's hand goes to his mouth, 'n' when an Injun does this, he's plenty astonished. All the tricks in the tracks are plain to 'em now. Some of 'em are hostile 'n' are for killin' him, but the old men of the party, say it is not good to kill a man whose tracks have fooled the hawk-eyed Ogallalys. Deformities amongst these people are few 'n' far between. In buildin' all wild animals, Nature makes few mistakes, Injuns 're only part human, 'n' when you see a cripple among 'em, it's safe bettin' that somebody's worked him over.

"They dont even wake Reel Foot, but coverin' their guns 'n' crawlin' their ponies, sneak away. When he raises from his nap he finds pony 'n' moccasin tracks, but never knows how close he comes to crossin' the range till about two years later, me 'n' him 's in a Ogallaly camp doin' some tradin'. We're in Blood Lance's lodge, smokin' 'n' dickerin' on this swap, when Blood Lance, who's been starin' at Reel Foot between puffs, lays down the pipe 'n' signs he knows him. 'Those feet,' says he, pointin' to Reel Foot's twisted legs, 'fooled the Ogallaly's 'n' saved the white man's hair, 'n' with that he spins us the yarn of Reel Foot's crooked tracks. Always after, he's knowed amongst the Ogallalys as 'The-Man-Who-Walks-Both-Ways.' "

Writer of legends.

Mormon Murphy's Confidence

THE LINE CAMP was jammed to her fifteen by twenty foot log walls. It was winter and the storm had driven many homeless punchers to shelter. Both bunks were loaded with loungers, and as cow-people never sit down when there is a chance to lie down, the blankets on the floor in their tarpaulin covers held their share of cigarette-smoking forms. Talk drifted from one subject to another—riding, roping, and general range chat, finally falling to the proper and handy way to carry a rifle.

"I used ter pack my gun in a sling," said old Dad Lane, the wolfer. "They ain't used these days, since men's got ter usin' scabbards 'n hangin' 'em under his legs. Them old-fashioned slings was used by all prairie and mountain men. If you never seed one, they was made of buckskin or sometimes boot leather, cut in what I'd call a long circle with a hole in each end that lipped over the saddle horn. The gun stuck through acrost in front of ye. In them same times men used gun-covers made of skin or blanket. As I said before, I used one of them slings till I near got caught with my hobbles on; since then I like my weapon loose an' handy. I'll tell you how the play comes up.

"It's back in '78, the same year that Joseph's at war agin the whites. Me an' Mormon Murphy's comin' up from Buford follerin' the Missouri, trappin' the streams an' headin toward Benton. This Murphy ain't no real Mormon. He's what we'd call a jack-Mormon; that is, he'd wintered down with Brigham an' played Mormon awhile. He's the best natured man I ever knowed, always wearin' a smile an' lookin' at the bright side of things. We'd wood-hawked, hunted an' trapped together for maybe four years, an' I never heered 'im kick on nothin'. He claims when a man's got his health he's got no license to belly-ache. Murphy's good-hearted till he's foolish, 'n' so honest he thinks everybody else is on the square. He says if you treat folks right, nobody'll bother you. It's a nice system to play, but I arger it won't do to gamble on. There is men that'll tell ye when ye've tipped yer hole card, but they're long rides apart. This same confidence in humans is what gets Mormon killed off.

"Well, as I said before, we're trappin' along 'n' takin' it easy. In them days all a man needs is a shootin'-iron 'n' a sack of salt to live. There's nothin' to worry us. We're in the Gros Ventres' country, but they ain't hoss-tile 'n' we're never out o'sight o'meat—the country's lousy with game.

"One mornin' we're joggin' along at a good gait. It's late in the fall 'n' ye know cool weather makes hosses travel up good, when ol' Blue, one of the pack-hosses, throws up his head 'n' straightens his ears like he sees something, 'n' when a hoss does this, ye can tap yerself, he ain't lyin'. So I go to watchin' the country ahead where he's lookin'.

"Sure enough, pretty soon there's a rider looms up out of a draw 'bout half a mile off. It's an Injun—I can tell by the way he swings his quirt 'n' is diggin' his heels in his pony's belly at every step. There's a skift of snow on the country 'n' he shows up plain agin the white. When he gits clost enough he throws up his hand 'n' signs he's a friend. Then I notice he's left-handed— anyhow, he's packin' his gun that-a-way. It's in a skin cover stuck through his belt, Injun fashion, with the stock to the left, but what looks crooked to me after sizin' him up is that his quirt hangs on his right wrist.

"With hand-talk I ask him what he is; he signs back Gros Ventre. This Injun looks like any other savage; he's wearin' a white blanket capote with blue leggins of the same goods. From the copper rim-fire cattridges in his belt, I guess his weapon's a Henry. Now what makes me think he's lyin' is his pony. He's ridin' a good-lookin' but leg-weary Appalusy, 'n', as I know, these hosses ain't bred by no Indians east o' the Rockies. 'Course all Injuns is good hoss-thieves, 'n' there's plenty o' chance he got him that-a-way, but the Umatilla camp's a long way off, 'n' these peculiar spotted ponies comes from either there or Nez Perce stock.

"Well, he rides up, 'n' instead o' comin' to my right 'n' facin' me, he goes

Me an' Mormon Murphy's comin' up from Buford follerin' the Missouri, headin' toward Benton.

roun' one o' the pack-hosses 'n' comes quarterin' behind me to the left, his hoss pintin' the same as mine, 'n' holdin out his hand, says, 'How!' with one o' them wooden smiles. Ye know ye can't tell what an Injun's got in his hole by readin' his countenance; winner or loser he looks the same. I shuk my head—someway I don't like this maneuver; I don't know what his game is, but ain't takin' no chances.

"He looks at me like his feelin's is hurt, swings around behind my hoss 'n' goes to Murphy the same way. Then I'm suspicious 'n' hollers to Murphy:
" 'Don't shake hands with that savage,' says I.

" 'What are ye afeared of?' says he, holdin' out his hand 'n smilin' good natured. 'He won't hurt nobody.' Them's the last words Mormon ever speaks.
"It's the quickest trick I ever seed turned; when they grip hands, that damn snake pulls Murphy toward him, at the same time, kickin' the Mormon's hoss in the belly. Naturally the animal lunges forward, makin' Murphy as helpless as a man with no arms. Like a flash the Injun's left hand goes under his gun-cover to the trigger. There's a crack 'n' the smell of burnt leather 'n' cloth.

"Murphy ain't hit the ground before that Injun quits his hoss, 'n' when he lands, he lands singin'. I savvy what that means—it's his death-song, 'n' I'm workin' like a beaver to loosen my gun from that damn sling. Maybe it ain't a second, but it seems to me like an hour before it's loose 'n' I'm playin' an accompaniment to his little ditty. This solo don't last long till I got him as quiet is he made the Mormon.

"When the Injun first rides up, he figgers on downin' me fust. He's a mind reader 'n' the smilin' Mormon looks easy. Seein' his game blocked, he takes a gamblin' chance. He'd a got me, too, but the lever on his Henry gets fowl of the fringe on the cover, 'n' I got him on a limb.

"Yes, I planted my pard, all right, but as I ain't got nothin' to dig a grave with bigger 'n a skinnin'-knife, I wraps him in his blanket 'n' packs him down to a washout 'n' caves a bank on him. When I takes a last look at him, he seems to be smilin' like he forgives everybody. I tell ye, fellers, I don't know when I cried, it's been a long time ago, 'n' I didn't shed no tears then, but I damn nigh choked to death at that funeral.

"I've helped plant a whole lot of men one time 'n' another in my career, but this is the only time I did it single-handed 'n' lonesmoe. It's just me 'n' the hosses, but I'll tell ye I'm damn glad to have them. When ye ain't got humans ye'll find animals good company.

"No, there ain't no prayers said; I ain't used none since I was weaned, 'n' I've forgot the little one my mammy learnt me! But, I figure it out this way, there ain't no use an old coyote like me makin' a squarin' talk for a man as good as Mormon Murphy. So I stand for a minut with my head bowed like whites do at funerals. It's the best I can do for him. Then I go to the hosses a-standin' there with their heads down like they're helpin' out as mourners, especially Murphy's with the empty saddle 'n' the gun still in the sling, pulled away off to one side where the helpless Mormon makes his last grab.

"I don't scalp the Injun—not that I wouldn't like to, but I ain't got time to gather no souvenirs 'n' I'm afeared to hang around, 'cause Injuns ain't lonesome animals; they band up, 'n' it's safe bettin' when we see one there's more near by. If I'd a tuk 'a' head and tail robe off'n him, I'd a peeled him to his dew-claws, but as it is I'm nervous 'n' hurried, 'n' all I got 's hoss 'n' gun 'n' four pair of new moccasins I found under his belt.

"Guess this Injun's a Nez Perce, all right, because a short time after the killin' of Murphy there's a bull-train jumped 'n' burned on the Cow Creek 'n' it ain't long till Joseph surrenders to Miles over on the Snake."

Noiseless conversation.

Night Herd

T HIS YARN, a friend of mine tells—I ain't givin' his name 'cause he's married and married men don't like history too near home, but I will say he's a cowpuncher and his folks on his mother's side wore moccasins. He tells me he's holding beef for the **TL** out of Big Sandy. Him and another cowpuncher is on night guard. I'll call this puncher "Big Man."

"We're holdin' about fifteen hundred out of Big Sandy," says Big. "We

I'm in the center of the town dump. The steers that I've been lookin' at are nothin' but stoves, tables an' all the discard of Sandy is there.

ain't more than two miles from town, expecting to load. Where we've got 'em bedded, you can see the lights of town, and once in a while I can hear singin' and music. It's a fine night. They've been on good grass all day and they're laying good, so good my pardner says to me, 'Big, if you want to go to town for a while, I'll hold 'em all right.' Says I, 'I won't be gone long, then you can take your turn.'

"It ain't long after till my hoss is at the rack, and I've joined the joy-makers. They're sure whooping her up, singin' and I get a little of that conversation fluid in me. I'm singin' so good, I wonder why some concert hall in Butte don't hire me. The bartender is busy as a beaver—the piano player's singin' 'Always take Mother's Advice; She Knows what is Best for Her Boy.' And, of course, we're all doin' that. I've heard that song where a rattlesnake would be ashamed to meet his mother. But whiskey is the juice of beautiful sentiment.

"A little while before I become unconscious I'm shaking hands with a feller that I knowed for years but never knowed he had a twin brother. The last I remember I'm crawling my horse at the rack. Then the light goes out. When I wake up I'm cold as a dead snake and I'm laying on my belly in the middle of the herd. I'm feared to move 'cause many of this bunch are out of the brakes an' are wild as buffalo and they're mighty touchy. If I'd get up, this bunch would beat me to it and when they've passed over, my friends would scrape me up with a hoe.

"I can't tell what time it is. It's cloudy and I can't find the dipper. There's one old spotted boy that I recognize—he's a seventy-nine steer. A few of them are standing. One I see is wanderin' around grazin', but they're mighty quiet. I'm gettin' colder every minute. I'm wantin' to smoke, but I dassn't. I put my head on my arm and doze a little, tain't long. The next time I take a look it's breaking day. And where do you think I am?" says Big Man.
"In the middle of the herd," says I.

"In the middle of the herd? In the middle of hell," says he. "I'm laying in the center of the town dump. The steers that I been looking at are nothing but stoves, tables, boxes, all the discard of Sandy is there. The few that's standin' are tables. That spotted seventy-nine steer that I know so well is a big goods box. Them spots is white paper. The one I see movin' around is my hoss. He's the only live thing in sight. I got a taste in my mouth like I had supper with a coyote. I ain't quite dead, but I wish I was. From where I am I can see Big Sandy and from the looks it's as near dead as I am."

Bulldogging a Steer.

Longrope's Last Guard

⁶⁶WHOEVER TOLD you that cattle stampede without cause was talkin'
like a shorthorn," says Rawhide. "You can bet all you got that whenever cattle run, there's a reason for it. A whole lot of times cattle
run, an' nobody knows why but the cows, an' they won't tell.

"There's plenty of humans call it instinct when an animal does something
they don't savvy. I don't know what it is myself, but I've seen the time when
I'd like to 'a' had some. I've knowed of hosses hein' trailed a thousand miles,
an' turned loose, that pulled back for their home range, not goin the trail they
come, but takin' cut-offs across mountain ranges that would puzzle a bighorn,
an' if you'd ask one of these wise boys how he done it, he'd back out of it easy
by sayin' it's instinct. Youll find cowponies that knows more about the business
than the men that rides 'em.

"There's plenty of causes for a stampede; sometimes it's a green hand or
a careless cowpuncher scratchin' a match to light a cigarette. Maybe it's something on the wind, or a tired night-hoss spraddles and stakes himself, an' the
poppin' of the saddle leather causes him to jump the bed ground. Scare a herd
on the start, and you're liable to have hell with them all the way. I've seen
bunches well trail-broke that you couldn't fog off the bed-ground with a slicker
an' six-shooter; others again, that had had a scare, you'd have to ride a hundred
yards away from to spit. Some men's too careful with their herd an' go tiptoein'
around like a mother with a sick kid. I've had some experience, an' claim this
won't do. Break 'em so they'll stand noise; get 'em used to seein' a man afoot,
an' you'll have less trouble.

"There's some herds that you dassent quit your hoss short of five hundred
yards of. Of course it's natural enough for a cow-brute that never see hoss
an' man apart to scare some when they see 'em separate. They think the top
of this ainmal's busted off, an' when they see the piece go movin' around they're
plenty surprised; but as I said before, there's many reasons for stampedes
unknown to man. I've seen herds start in broad daylight with no cause that
anybody knows of. The smell of blood will start 'em goin'; this generally
come off in the mornin' when they're quittin' the bed-ground. Now, in every
herd you'll find steers that's regular old rounders. They won't go to bed like
decent oflks, but put in the night perusin' around, disturbin' the peace. If
there's any bulls in the bunch, there's liable to be fightin'. I've often watched
an old bull walkin' around through the herd an' talkin' fight, hangin' up his
bluff, with a bunch of these rounders at his heels. They're sure backin' him
up—boostin' an' ribbin' up trouble, an' if there's a fight pulled off you should
hear these trouble-builders takin' sides; every one of 'em with his tongue out
an' his tail kinked, buckin' an' bellerin, like his money's all up. These night
ramblers that won't go to bed at decent hours, after raisin' hell all night, are
ready to bed down an' are sleepin' like drunks when decent cattle are walkin'
off the bed-ground.

"Now, you know, when a cow-brute quits his bed he bows his neck, gaps
an' stretches all the same as a human after a night's rest. Maybe he accident-
ally tromps on one of these rounder's tail that's layin' along the ground. This

They're all plumb hog-wild an' if you want any beef left in your herd, you'd better cut out the one that's causin' the excitement.

hurts plenty, and Mr. Night Rambler ain't slow about wakin' up; he raises like he's overslept an' 's afeared he'll miss the coach, leavin' the tossel of his tail under the other fellow's hoof. He goes off wringin' his stub an' scatterin' blood on his rump an' quarters. Now the minute them other cattle winds the blood, the ball opens. Every hoof 's at his heels barkin' and bellerin'. Them that's close enough are hornin' him in the flank like they'd stuck to finish him off. They're all plumb hog-wild, an' if you want any beef left in your herd, you'd better cut out the one that's causin' the excitement, 'cause an hour of this will take off more taller than they'll put on in a month.

"Cattle like open country to sleep in; I sure hate to hold a herd near any brakes or deep 'royos, 'cause no matter how gentle a herd is, let a coyote or any other animal loom up of a sudden close to 'em an' they don't stop to take a second look, but are gone like a flash in the pan. Old bulls comin' up without talkin' sometimes jump a herd this way, an' it pays a cowpuncher to sing when he's comin' up out of a 'royo close to the bed-ground.

"Some folks'll tell you that cowboys sing their cows to sleep, but that's a mistake, judgin' from my experience, an' I've had some. The songs an' voices I've heard around cattle ain't soothin'. A cowpuncher sings to keep himself company; it aint that he's got any motherly love for these longhorns he's put to bed an' 's ridin' herd on; he's amusin' himself an' nobody else. These ditties are generally shy on melody an' strong on noise. Put a man alone in the dark, an if his conscience is clear an' he ain't hidin' he'll sing an' don't need to be a born vocalist. Of course singin's a good thing around a herd an' all punchers know it. In the darkness it lets the cows know where you're at. If you ever woke up in the darkness an' found somebody—you didn't know who or what— loomin' up over you, it would startle you, but if this somebody is singin' or whistlin', it wouldn't scare you none. It's the same wth Mr. Steer; that snaky, noiseless glidin' up on him's what scares the animal.

"All herds has some of these lonesomes that won't lie down with the other cattle, but beds down alone maybe twenty-five to thirty yards from the edge of the herd. He's got his own reason for this; might be he's short an eye. This bein' the case you can lay all you got he's layin' with the good blinker next to the herd. He don't figure on lettin' none of his playful brothers beef his ribs from a sneak. One-eyed hoss is the same. Day or night you'll find him on the outside with his good eye watchin' the bunch. Like Mister Steer the confidence he's got in his brother's mighty frail.

"But these lonesome cattle I started to tell you about is the ones that a puncher's most liable to run onto in the dark, layin' out that way from the herd. If you ride onto him singin' it don't startle Mr. Steer; he raises easy, holdin' his ground till you pass; then he lays down in the same place. He's got the ground warm an' hates to quit her. Cows, the same as humans, like warm beds. Many's the time in cool weather I've seen some evil-minded, low-down steer stand around like he ain't goin' to bed, but all the time, he's got his eye on some poor, undersized brother layin' near by, all innocent. As soon as he thinks the ground's warm he walks over, horns him out an' jumps his claim. This low-down trick is sometimes practiced by punchers when they got a gentle herd. It don't hurt a cowpuncher's conscience none to sleep in a bed he stole from a steer.

"If you ride sneakin' an' noiseless onto one of these lonesome fellers, he gets right to his feet with dew-claws an' hoofs rattlin', an' 's runnin' before he's half up, hittin' the herd like a canned dog, an', quicker than you can bat an eye, the whole herd's gone. Cow are slow animals, but scare 'm an' they're fast enough; a thousand will get to their feet as quick as one. It's sure a puzzler to cowmen to know how a herd will all scare at once, an' every animal will get on his feet at the same time. I've seen herds do what a cowpuncher would call jump—that is to raise an' not run. I've been lookin' across a herd in bright moonlight—a thousand head or more, all down; with no known cause there's a short, quick rumble, an' every hoof's standin'.

"I've read of stampedes that were sure dangerous an' scary, where a herd would run through a camp upsettin' wagons an' trompin' sleepin' cowpunchers to death. When day broke they'd be fifty or a hundred miles from where they started, leavin' a trail strewn with blood, dead cowpunchers an' hosses, that looked like the work of a Kansas cyclone. This is all right in books, but the feller that writes 'em is romancin' an' don't savvy the cow. Most stampedes is noisy, but harmless to anybody but the cattle. A herd in a bad storm might drift thirty miles in a night, but the worst run I ever see, we ain't four miles from the bed-ground when the day broke.

"This was down in Kansas; we're trailin' beef an' have got about seventeen hundred head. Barrin' a few dry ones the herd's straight steers, mostly Spanish longhorns from down on the Cimaron. We're about fifty miles south of Dodge. Our herd's well broke an' lookin' fine, an' the cowpunchers all good-natured, thinkin' of the good time comin' in Dodge.

"That evenin' when we're ropin' our hosses for night guard, the trail boss, 'Old Spanish,' we call him (he ain't no real Spaniard, but he's rode some in old Mexico an' can talk some Spanish), says to me: 'Them cattle ought to hold well; they ain't been off water four hours an' we grazed 'em plumb onto the bed-ground. Every hoof of 'em 's got a paunch full of grass an' water, an' that's what makes cattle lay good.'

"Me an a feller called Longrope's on first guard. He's a center-fire or single-cinch man from California; packs a sixty-foot rawhide riata, an' when he takes her down an' runs about half of her into a loop she looks big, but when it reaches the animal, comes pretty near fittin' hoof or horn. I never went much on these long-rope boys, but this man comes as near puttin' his loop where he wants as any I ever see. You know Texas men ain't got much love for a single rig, an' many's the argument me an Longrope has on this subject. He claims a center-fire is the only saddle, but I 'low that they'll do all right on a shad-bellied western hoss, but for Spanish pot-gutted ponies they're no good. You're ridin' up on his withers all the time.

"When we reach the bed-ground most of the cattle's already down, lookin' comfortable. They're bedded in open country, an' things look good for an easy night. It's been mighty hot all day, but there's a little breeze now makin' it right pleasant; but down the west I notice some nasty-lookin' clouds hangin' round the new moon that's got one horn hooked over the skyline, an' so far off that you can just hear her rumble, but she's walkin' up on us slow, an' I'm hopin' she'll go round. The cattle's all layin' quiet an' nice, so me an' Longrope stop to talk awhile.

"'They're layin' quiet,' says I.'

"'Too damn quiet,' says he. 'I like cows to lay still all right, but I want some of the natural noises that goes with a herd this size. I want to hear 'em blowin' off, an' the creakin' of their joints, showin' they're easin' themselves in their beds. Listen, an' if you hear anything I'll eat that rimfire saddle of yours—grass rope an' all.'

"I didn't notice till then, but when I straighten my ears it's quiet as a grave. An' if it ain't for the lightnin' showin' the herd once in a while, I couldn't 'a' believed that seventeen hundred head of longhorns lay within forty feet of where I'm sittin' on my hoss. It's gettin' darker every minute, an' if it wasn't for Longrope's slicker I couldn't 'a' made him out, though he's so close I could have touched him with my hand. Finally it darkens up so I can't see him at all. It's black as a nigger's pocket; you couldn't find your nose with both hands.

"I remember askin' Longrope the time.

" 'I guess I'll have to get help to find the timepiece,' says he, but gets her after feelin' over himself, an' holdin' her under his cigarette takes a long draw, lightin' up her face.

" 'Half-past nine,' says he.

" 'Half an hour more,' I says. 'Are you goin' to wake up the next guard or did you leave it to the hoss-wrangler?'

" 'There won't be but one guard to-night' he answers, 'an' we'll ride it. You might as well hunt for a hoss-thief in heaven as look for that camp. Well, I guess I'll mosey 'round'; an' with that he quits me.

"The lightnin' 's playin' every little while. It ain't makin' much noise, but lights up enough to show where you're at. There ai'nt no use ridin', by the flashes I can see that every head's down. For a second it'll be like broad day, then darker than the dungeons of hell, an' I notice the little fire-balls on my hoss's ears; when I spit there's a streak in the air like strikin' a wet match. These little fire-balls is all I can see of my hoss, an' they tell me he's listenin' all ways; his ears are never still.

"I tell you, there's something mighty ghostly about sittin' up on a hoss you can't see, with them two little blue sparks out in front of you wigglin' an' movin' like a pair of spook eyes, an' it shows me the old night hoss is usin' his listeners pretty plenty, I got my ears cocked, too, hearing nothin' but Longrope's singin'; he's easy three hundred yards across the herd from me, but I can hear every word:—

'Sam Bass was born in Injiana,
It was his native home,
'Twas at the age of seventeen
Young Sam began to roam.
He first went out to Texas,
A cowboy for to be;
A better hearted feller
You'd seldom ever see.'

"It's so plain it sounds like he's singin' in my ear; I can even hear the click-clack of his spur chains against his stirrups when he moves 'round, an' the cricket in his bit—he's usin' one of them hollow conchoed half-breeds—she comes plain to me in the stillness. Once there's a steer layin' on the edge of the herd starts sniffin'. He's takin' long draws of the air he's nosin' for something. I don't like this, it's a bad sign; it shows he's layin' for trouble, an' all he needs is some little excuse.

"Now every steer, when he beds down, holds his breath for a few seconds, then blows off; that noise is all right an' shows he's settlin' himself for comfort. But when he curls his nose an' makes them long draws it's a sign he's sniffin' for something, an' if anything crosses his wind that he don't like there's liable to be trouble. I've seen dry trail herds mighty thirsty, layin' good till a breeze springs off the water, maybe ten miles away; they start sniffin', an' the minute they get the wind you could comb Texas an' wouldn't have enough punchers to turn 'em till they wet their feet an' fill the paunches.

"I get tired sittin' there starin' at nothin' so start ridin' 'round. Now it's sure dark when animals can't see, but I tell you by the way my hoss moves he's feelin' his way, but I don't blame him none; it's like lookin' in a black pot. Sky an' ground all the same, an' I ain't gone twenty-five yards till I hear cattle gettin' up around me; I'm in the herd an' it's luck I'm singing an' they don't get scared Pullin' to the left I work cautious an easy till I'm clear of the bunch. Ridin's useless, so I flop my weight over on one stirrup an' go on singin'.

"The lightnin' 's quit now an' she's darker than ever; the breeze has died down an' it's hotter than the hubs of hell. Above my voice I can hear Longrope. He's singin' the 'Texas Ranger' now; the Ranger's a long song an' there's few punchers that knows it all, but Longrope's sprung a lot of new verses on me an' I'm interested. Seems like he's on about the twenty-fifth verse, an' there's danger of his chokin' down, when there's a whisperin' in the grass behind me; it's a breeze sneakin' up. It flaps the tail of my slicker an' goes by; in another second she hits the herd. The ground shakes an' they're all runnin'. My hoss takes the scare with 'em an' 's bustin' a hole in the darkness when he throws both front feet in a badger hole, goin to his knees an' plowin his nose in the dirt. But he's a good night hoss an' 's hard to keep down. The minute he gets his feet under him he raises, runnin' like a scared wolf. Hearin' the roar behind him he don't care to mix with them locoed longhorns. I got my head turned over my shoulder listenin', tryin' to make out which way they're goin' when there's a flash of lightnin' busts a hole in the sky—it's one of these kind that puts the fear of God in a man, thunder an' all together. My hoss whirls an' stops in his tracks, spraddlin' out an' squattin' like he's hit, an' I can feel his heart beatin agin my leg, while mine's poundin' my ribs like it'll bust through. We're both plenty scared.

"This flash lights up the whole country, givin' me a glimpse of the herd runnin' a little to my left. Big drops of rain are pounding on my hat. The storm has broke now for sure with the lightnin' bombardin' us at every jump. Once a flash shows me Longrope, ghostly in his wet slicker. He's so close to me that I could hit him with my quirt an' I hollers to him :—

" 'This is hell.'

" 'Yes,' he yells back above the roar; 'I wonder what damned fool kicked the lid off.'

"I can tell by the noise that they're runnin' straight; there ain't no clickin' of horns. It's a kind of hummin' noise like a buzz-saw, only a thousand times louder. There's no use in tryin' to turn 'em in this darkness, so I'm ridin' wide—just herdin' by ear an' follerin' the noise. Pretty soon my ears tell me they're crowdin' an' comin' together; the next flash shows em all millin', with heads jammed together an' horns locked; some's rared up ridin' others an' these is squirmin' like bristled snakes. In the same light I see Longrope, an' from the blink I get of him he's among 'em or too close for safety, an' in the dark I thought I saw a gun flash three times with no report, but with the noise these longhorns are makin' now, I doubt if I could 'a' heard a six-gun bark if I pulled the trigger myself, an' the next thing I know me an' my hoss goes over a bank, lightin' safe. I guess it ain't over four feet, but it seems like fifty in the darkness, an' if it hadn't been for my chin-string I'd a' went from under my hat. Again the light shows me we're in a 'royo with the cattle comin' over the edge, wigglin' an' squirmin' like army worms.

"It's a case of all night riding. Sometimes they'll mill an' quiet down, then start trottin' an' break into a run. Not till daybreak do they stop, an' maybe you think old day ain't welcome. My hoss is sure leg-weary, an' I ain't so rollicky myself. When she gets light enough I begin lookin' for Longrope, with nary a sign of him; an' the herd, you wouldn't know they were the same cattle—smeared with mud an' ga'nt as greyhounds; some of 'em with their tongues still lollin' out from their night's run; but sizin' up the bunch I guess I got 'em all. I'm kind of worried about Longrope. It's a cinch that wherever he is he's afoot, an' chances is he's layin' on the prairie with a broken leg.

"The cattle's spread out an' they begin feedin'. There ain't much chance of losin' 'em, now it's broad daylight, so I ride up on a raise to take a look at the back trail. While I'm up there viewin' the country, my eyes run onto somethin' a mile back in a draw. I can't make it out, but get curious, so spurrin' my tired hoss into a lope I take the back trail. 'Tain't no trouble to foller in the mud; it's plain as plowed ground. I ain't rode three hundred yard till the country raises a little an' shows me this thing's a hoss, an' by the white streak on his flank I heap savy it's Peon—that's the hoss Longrope's ridin'. When I get close he whinners pitiful like; hes lookin' for sympathy, an' I notice, when he turns to face me, his right foreleg's broke. He's sure a sorry sight with that fancy, full-stamped center-fire saddle hangin' under his belly in the mud. While I'm lookin' him over, my hoss cocks his ears to the right, snortin' low. This scares me—I'm afeared to look. Somethin' tells me I won't see Longrope, only part of him— that part that stays here on earth when the man's gone. Bracin' up, I foller my hoss's ears, an' there in the holler of the 'royo is a patch of yeller; it's part of a slicker. I spur up to get a better look over the bank, an' there tromped in the mud is all there is left of Longrope. Pullin' my gun I empty her in the air. This brings the boys that are follerin' on the trail from the bed-ground. Nobody 'd had to tell 'em we'd had hell, so they come in full force, every man but the cook an' hoss-wrangler.

"Nobody feels like talkin'. It don't matter how rough men are,—I've known 'em that never spoke without cussin', that claimed to fear neither God, man, nor devil,—but let death visit camp an' it puts 'em thinkin'. They generally take their hats off to this old boy that comes everywhere an' any time. He's always ready to pilot you—willin' or not—over the long dark trail that folks don't care to travel. He's never welcome, but you've got to respect him.

" 'It's tough—damned tough,' says Spanish, raisin' poor Longrope's head.an' wipin the mud from his face with his neck-handkerchief, tender, like he's feared he'll hurt him. We find his hat tromped in the mud not fur from where he's layin' His scabbard 's empty an' we never do locate his gun.

"That afternoon when we're countin' out the herd to see if we're short any, we find a steer with a broken shoulder an' another with a hole plumb through his nose. Both these is gun wounds; this accounts for them flashes I see in the night. It looks like, when Longrope gets mixed in the mill, he tries to gun his way out, but the cattle crowd him to the bank an' he goes over. The chances are he was dragged from his hoss in a tangle of horns.

"Some's for takin' him to Dodge an' gettin' a box made for him, but Old Spanish says: 'Boys, Longrope is a prairie man, an' if she was a little rough at times, she's been a good foster mother. She cared for him while he's awake, let her nurse him in his sleep.' So we wrappd him in his blankts, an' put him to bed.

"It's been twenty years or more since we tucked him in with the end-gate of the bed-wagon for a headstone, which the cattle have long since rubbed down, leavin' the spot unmarked. It sounds lonesome, but he ain't alone, 'cause these old prairies has cradled many of his kind in their long sleep."

How Lindsay Turned Indian

"**M**OST folks don't bank much on squaw-men, but I've seen some mighty good ones doubled up with she Injuns," says Dad Lane, "ain't you, Owens?"

"I told you my short experience with that Blood woman; I wasn't a successful Injun, but the comin' of white women to the country's made big changes; men's got finicky about matin'. I guess if I'd come to the country earlier, squaws would 'a' looked good enough, an' if there wasn't nothin but Injun women, its a cinch that all married men would be wearin' moccasins. There's a whole lot of difference livin' with Injuns now an' when the buffalo were thick; the savages owned the country then.

"When I'm riding' line for the H-half-H, my camp's on the border of the Piegan Reserve. Of course I gets lots of visits from my red brothers. Among 'em is an old squaw-man named Lindsay. He's white all right, but you'd have to be a good guesser to call the turn. Livin' so long with Injuns, he's got all their ways an' looks. Can't talk without usin' his hands. His white hair's down over his shoulder an' his wrinkled face is hairless. By the holes punched in his ears I know he's wore rings sometimes. He packs a medicine-bag, all same savage.

"From his looks an' the dates he gives me, he's crowdin' eighty winters. This old boy could string the best war and buffalo yarns I ever heard. It's like readin' a romance; any time he calls I'm sure of a good yarn.

"I remember one day we're sittin' outside the shack, clear of the eaves. There's a Chinook blowing an' the roof 's drippin' like it's rainin'. It's mighty pleasant in the sun out of the wind. This old breeze is cuttin' the snow off the hills in a way that's a blessin' to cows an' cowmen. The country 's been hid for six weeks, an' if the Chinook hadn't come, cowmen would needed skinnin'-knives instead of brandin'-irons.

"As I said before, we're sittin' outside enjoyin' the change; the white Injun's smokin' his mixture of willow bark an tobacco, while I'm sizin' him up, an' somehow I can't help but pity him. Here's an old man as white as I am. No doubt he's been a great man with these savages, but he's nothin' or nobody to his own blood an' color. While I'm thinkin' about him in this way he starts mumblin' to himself in Injun. I don't savvy only part of it, so I ask him what it's all about. He says he's talkin' to the sun; he's thankin' him for the warm wind that melts the snow.

" 'Don't you believe in God?' says I.

" 'Yes,' says he.

" 'What kind of a one?'

"That one,' says he, pintin' with his staff to the sun. 'The one I can see an' have watched work for many years. He gathers the clouds an' makes it rain; then warms the ground an' the grass turns green. When it's time he dries it yellow, makin' it good winter feed for grass-eaters.'

At the top of the ridge the herd shows—a couple of thousand, all spread an' grazin'. But seein' these red hunters pilin' down on 'em, their heads leave the grass. One look's a plenty, an' with tails straightened, they start lumberin' together. It ain't long till they've bunched, millin' and churnin', all same spotted cattle.

" 'Again, when he's mad, my people say, he drives the rain away, dryin' up the streams an' water-holes. If it wasn't for him there couldn't nothin' or nobody live. Do you wonder that we pray him to be good an' thank him when he is? I'm all Injun but my hide; their God 's my God, an' I don't ask for no better.'

" 'However did you come to throw in with these savages in the start-off,' says I.

" 'Well, boy, I'll tell you how it happened,' says he, signin' for a match, an', lightin' up fresh, he starts off.

"There used to be lots of white Injuns like me—what you'd call squaw-men, but I've outlived the most of 'em. Some got civilized, throwed away their red women an' took white ones, but I've been too long in the Piegan camp to change, an', nearin' the end o' the road like I am, I guess Ill finish with the red ones.

" 'Its the women that make the men in this world, I heard an educated feller say once, an' it's the truth that, if a man 's goin' to hell or heaven, if you look in the trail ahead of him, you'll find a track the same shape as his, only smaller; its a woman's track. She's always ahead, right or wrong, tollin' him on. In animals, the same as humans, the female leads. That ain't the exact words this educated man uses, but it's as near as I can interpret, 'n' it's the truth. If you ever run buffalo, you'll notice the cow-meats in the lead. With wild hosses the stallion goes herdin' them along, snakin' an' bowin' his neck, with his tail flagged. From looks you'd call him chief, but the mares lead to the water-hole they've picked out. An' I believe, if all women were squaws, the whites would be wearin' clouts to-day.

" 'In early times when white men mixed with Injuns away from their own kind, these wild women, in their paint an' beads, looked mighty enticin', but to stand in with a squaw you had to turn Injun. She'd ask were your relations all dead that you cut your hair? or was you afraid the enemy'd get a hold an' lift it?—at the same time givin' you the sign for raisin' the scalp. The white man, if he liked the squaw, wouldn't stand this joshin' ling till he throwed the shears away an' by the time the hair reached his shoulders, he could live without salt. He ain't long forgettin' civilization. Livin' with nature an' her people this way, he goes backwards till he's a raw man, without any flavorin'. In grade, he's a notch or two above a wolf, follerin' the herds for his meat the same as his wild dog-brother. But, boy, I started to tell you about myself,' an' this is about the way he strings it to me.

"He's born in St. Louis, at that time the outfittin'-place for all fur trade south of the British line. His first remembrance, when he's a youngster, is seein' traders in from their far-off, unknown country. These long-haired fellers, some in fringed buckskin, others in bright-colored blanket-clothes, strike the kid's fancy. There's Frenchmen an' Breeds that's come down in boats loaded with buffalo an' beaver hides, from the upper Missouri. From the Southwest comes the Spanish an' Mexican traders, their hundreds of pack-mules loaded with pelts. These men are still more gaudy, with silver braid an' buttons from their broad sombreros to their six-inch rowels, all wearin' bright-colored sashes an' serapis. Sometimes a band of Pawnees would drift in from the plains, their faces painted an' heads shaved, barrin' the scalplock.

"All these sights make this romantic kid restless, an' it wouldn't take much to make him break away. So one day a tannin' he gets from his step-dad gives him all the excuse he needs, an' bustin' home ties, he quits the village as fast as his small feet an' shanks will pack him. Follerin' the Mississippi he's mighty leg-weary an' hungry next mornin' when he meets up with Pierre Chouteau's cordellers or boatmen. He tells 'em his story between whimpers an' tears, an' these big-hearted river travelers feed him an' take him in.

"They're about the mouth of the Missouri when he overtakes 'em, towin' north with goods for the Upper Missouri trade. This trip ain't no picnic, but bein' a strong, healthy kid, he enjoys it. They pass the dirt-lodge towns of the Mandans an' Rickarees, that look like overgrown anthills, where the Injuns come to meet 'em in bowl-shaped bull-boats, made of green buffalo hide, stretched on willers. Many times they're stopped by herds of buffalo crossin' the river. It's pretty smooth for the kid, chorin' around an' herdin' hosses for the post, till one day he falls asleep an' a war-party of Crows drop down an' get about half of 'em. This makes the chief of the post hostile, an' he has Lindsay licked. This old man tells me that the chiefs of tradin'- posts made their own laws, an' when you broke one you had a floggin' comin'. Sometimes men were shot or hung, accordin' to how serious the break was. The lickin' he gets is too much for him, so he busts out an' makes a get-away.

"There's about a hundred lodges of Piegans pullin' north, camped two mile above the post. He finds out these Injuns will break camp about daybreak. It's gettin' gray when he clears the stockade. On reachin' the camp-ground he's mighty disappointed in findin' nothin' but the dead ashes of their fires. He's afraid to go back to the post, an' the Missouri lays between him an' the Injuns, so bein' desperate, he strips his garments an' takes the water. Before startin' he ties his clothes in a pack on his shoulders.

"The water's low an' don't require much swimmin', but nearin' the bank on the fur side, an undercurrent catches him an' he loses his gun. This old flintlock is mighty dear to him, but it's a case of lighten up or go under, so he loosens his holt, hittin' the shore with nothin' but a wet powder-horn an' a skinnin'-knife. The draggin' of hundreds of travoys an' lodge-poles makes a trail as easy to foller as a wagon road. About noon he reaches the rear guard. In them days Injuns traveled, when in dangerous country, with advance, flank, an' rear guard, their squaws, children, an' loose ponies in the centre. The Piegans, bein' in the Sioux country, ain't takin' no chances.

"When he meets up with the rear guard they're down off their ponies, figurin' on a smoke, but they've lost the steel an' there don't happen to be a flintlock gun in this bunch. They're tryin' hard to get a light by hackin' an old iron trade knife agin the flint. When Lindsay looms up, Injun-like, they don't hardly notice him. These months around the post, he's picked up considerable hand-talk, so signs 'em he'll light their pipe. One old pock-marked buck, that's holdin' the pipe an' seems to be chief, says, 'The boy is foolish, if he has no steel, to talk to old men.'

"Lindsay don't make no back talk, but, walkin' up to the old man signs him to hold the bowl up; that the sun will make smoke. Then, reachin' in his pouch, he pulls a sun-glass. As I says before, it's about noon an' the sun's well up, It's one of them warm fall days, not a cloud in the sky; this makes it easy for Lindsay, so holdin' the glass above the bowl an' movin' her up an' down till he gets the focus, an' holdin her steady, its not long before the little bright light down in the bowl sends up a fine curl of smoke. The old Injun, seein' this, takes a long draw, an' when they all see the smoke roll from the old chief's nostrils they're plenty surprised, but don't show it none; 'tain't Injun nature. You could take one of these savages up to the Missouri river an' by a wave of your hand stop the flow an' back her up a mile, an' if he didn't want to, he wouldn't change expression; he wouldn't even look interested. His old insides might be boilin' with astonishment, but you'd never know it. On these people it don't show through the hide.

"When they get through passin' the pipe, they all fork their ponies, an' the old Injun signs the kid to crawl up behind him on his pony. He's pretty leg-weary an' don't wait for no second invite, so rides double the rest of the way with the old man. By the time they reach camp the news is spread 'round about the medicine-boy that lights the pipe with the sun. He can hardly eat his supper for Injuns crowdin' around takin' a peek at him. The young women look at him, the old hags kiss him, an' the mothers rub their papooses on his breast to get his medicine. Lindsay takes it all good-humored, barrin' the old ladies kissin' him, which he says don't mix well with his supper. That night Lindsay tells the old man how the trader treated him an' begs not to be sent back.

"This old Injun, Wounded Hoss is his name, is chief of the band. He tells the boy he'll not be sent back an' there's no danger of the trader follerin' him, for a white man that follers a Piegan those days, unless he's lookin' for trouble, is plumb silly.

" 'The grass has grown twice since my two sons were killed by the Sioux,' says the old chief; 'my heart is on the ground; I am lonesome, but since the sun has sent you, it is good. I will adopt you as my boy. I am old an' my muscles are tired—very tired. My lodge is yours till you're old enough to take a woman. I have plenty ponies, an' among them good buffalo hosses. You shall ride them, an' bring meat an' robes to my women. Child of the Sun it is good'; an' after that, until Lindsay won his war-name, he was known as 'Child of the Sun.'

"Next day his new father gives him a bow an' otter-skin quiver, filled with steel-pointed arrows. This bow is of fine make, chockecherry wood, wrapped with sinew. With this rig, mounted on a fine pinto, this kid wouldn't trade places with the President.

"The first few days there ain't nothin' happens; Lindsay rides along with the bunch, learnin' to handle the bow. This ain't no easy trick, for though a bow with a Injun behind it's a nasty weapon, with a green hand it's mighty near harmless. It takes an expert to pull an arrow back to the head, an' it's several years before Lindsay can get the knack an' can drive his arrow to the feathers. The Injun pulls his string with three an' sometimes four fingers, with all his strength, an' by gettin' back of the ribs, an' aimin' forward, he'll drive his arrow plumb to the lungs an' sometimes clean through a buffalo.

"Lindsay's enjoyin' the life fine, barrin' his everlastin' longin' for salt an' sugar. He craves it all day an' dreams of it nights, an it's months before he's plumb weaned.

"About the fourth evenin' some scouts ride in with news of a big herd they've located a short ride north of 'em, so all hands prepare for a surround next day. The kid's so excited he don't sleep much. All night long he can hear the tom-tom of the medicine-man. It's just breakin' day when he wakes. Everybody an' the dogs are up. Quittin' the pile of robes he throws the lodge door aside. The ponies are among the lodges; squaws an' bucks are all busy pickin' out their mounts. From the fires in front of the lodges he can smell meat cookin'.

Lookin' around he spies his foster father wrapped to his eyes in his robes. He don't recognize him in the dim light till he speaks.

" 'My son, bring your rope an' foller me,' says Wounded Hoss.

"Gettin' his rawhide, Lindsay follers the old man among the ponies, an' after two or three throws, gets his loop over a black pinto that is pointed out to him as his buffalo hoss.

"While they're eatin', one of the kid's foster mothers leads up three more ponies. One of these is for Wounded Hoss; the other for his adopted boy. Injuns generally led their buffalo hosses to the runnin' ground, an' that's what these extra mounts is for. In them days buffalo hosses was worth plenty of robes. This animal had to be sure-footed, long-winded an' quick as a cat. It's no bench of a hoss that'll lay alongside of a buffalo cow, while you're droppin' arrows or lead in her. He's got to be a dodger, all the same cow-hoss, cause a wounded cow's liable to get ringy or on the fight, an' when she does, she's mighty handy with them black horns. An Injun's sure proud of his buffalo hoss, an' this animal gets the best a savage can give 'em. Old Lindsay tells me, in winters, when its a bad storm, he's seen 'em put the ponies in the lodges an' the squaws would bring grass that they cut with their knives or a kind of hoe that they had for that purpose.

"This white Injun tells me that if he lives a thousand years, he'll never forget that day. Just this bunch of riders is a sight worth seein.' There's about two hundred bucks, youngsters an' all, an' ponies—well, there ain't no color known to hossflesh that ain't there. Some of 'em's painted till you couldn't tell what shade of hide he wears. Each buck's ridin' an ordinary-lookin' cayuse, but the one he's leadin', or's got a light boy ridin' is sure gay an' gaudy, with tail an' foretop tied up an' decked with feathers. Maybe he's got a medicine-bag hangin' in his mane to make him strong an' lucky. Paint's smeared regardless an' there's pictures all over him.

"Barrin' some old coffee-cooler mumblin' a prayer, or a pony clearin' his nostrils, these riders are joggin' along pretty near as noiseless as a band of ghosts. Barefoot ponies on well-grassed sod travel mighty silent, an' the savages ain't doin' no talkin' except with their hands. This is where sign-talk comes in mighty handy. In quiet weather the mumble of a dozen men will travel for miles, but with hand-talk a thousand Injuns might be within gunshot an' you'd never know it. Buffalo, like most four-footed animals, are wind-readers, but there ain't nothin' the matter with their hearin', so, after gettin' the wind right, Mr. Injun makes a sneak, an' there aint nobody capable of givin' him lessons in the art of hidin' or sneakin'. It's been proved; for years they've played 'I-spy' with Uncle Sam, an' most of the time Uncle's been 'It'.

"They ain't gone four miles when a scout looms up on a butte an' signs with his robe. This signal causes them all to spread out an' every Injun slides from his pony an' starts backin' out of his cowskin shirt an' skinnin' his leggins. 'Tain't a minute till they're all stripped to the clout an' moccasins, forkin' their ponies, naked like themselves barrin' two half hitches of rawhide on the lower jaw. That sign means that the herd is in sight an' close. When they're all mounted, the scout on the butte swings his robe a couple of times around his head an' drops it. Before it hits the ground every pony's runnin, with a red rider quirtin' him down the hind leg, leavin' little curls of dust in the yellow dust behind him. At the top of the ridge the herd shows—a couple of thousand, all spread out grazin'. But seein' these red hunters pilin' down on 'em, their heads leave the grass. One look's a plenty, an' with tails straightened, they start lumberin' together. It ain't long till they've bunched, millin' an' churnin', all same spotted cattle.

"When Lindsay gets to 'em, the dust's rollin' so he just gets a glimpse now an' again of his naked brothers emptyin' their quivers. He notices Mr. Injun pull five or six arrows at a draw, holdin' the extras in his mouth an' bow-hand, an' the way he's got of turnin' 'em loose don't trouble him none. Above the rumble an' gruntin' of these animals, he faintly hears now an' agin the reports of a fuke, or sawed-off flintlock, or the quick, sharp yelp of the Injun, as he sends his arrow home. Barrin' this, it's all dust an' rumblin'. Lindsay singles out a cow for his meat. The dodgin' of his pony mighty near unloads him, but by hookin' his toe under the fore leg, Injun fashion, he manages to keep his hoss under him. The kid gets the cow all right, but he tells me she resembles a porcupine; her hide's bristlin' with arrows when she lays down. After the run's over, they've made a killin' of about three hundred, While the squaws are skinnin', Lindsay lunches on raw liver, like any other Injun. Looks like this short run has turned his savage.

" 'My boy,' says Lindsay, finishin' up his yarn, openin' an' shuttin' his hands like an Injun, I savvy he's countin' winters,—'that's been sixty-five years ago as near as I can figure. I run buffalo till the whites cleaned 'em out, but that's the day I turned Injun, an' I ain't cut my hair since.' "

In quiet weather the mumble of a dozen men will travel for miles, but with hand-talk a thousand Injuns might be within gunshot an' you'd never know it.

Hands Up!

JACK SHEA tells one time about being held up. It was in Colorado, and he's travelin' on a coach. There's five passengers and one of them is a middle-aged woman. There's been a lot of stick-up men on this road, and this old lady is worried. She's got fifty dollars and she's tryin' to get to her daughter some where up north. This fifty is all she's got, and if she loses it she's on the rocks.

There's an old man in the bunch that's got all the earmarks of a cowman. He tells her to stick her roll under the chusions, and slips her a couple of dollars, sayin' that it will pacify these road robbers.

"We ain't gone five mile when the coach stops sudden and a gent outside says, 'step out folks, an' keep your hands up while you're doin' it.' We all know what we're up against and ain't slow gettin' out. There's one gent at the leaders, got the driver and the outside passenger covered; another that's waitin' for us. They're both wearin' blinds and heeled till they look nasty. This stick-up seems to know the old cowman and speaks to him. The old man steps out of line and whispers something to him. None of us get any of his talk, but when the hold-up gets through trimmin' us he reaches into the coach, flips the cushion, and grabs the old lady's roll. Then we all return to our seats and the hold-up gives the driver his orders and the coach pulls out.

"We're all trimmed; the old lady's cryin', and the rest of us ain't sayin' much, but we're doin' lots of thinkin'. From what we get, it looks like the old cowman stands in with the hold-ups. He's tellin' the lady not to take it so hard. When one of the passengers wants to know what the low talk is between him and the stick-up, the cowman don't turn a hair but tells us all he double-crossed the lady; that he tells this hold-up that twenty dollars is his bank roll, but if he'll pass him up he knows where there's fifty. The hold-up agrees, and he tips off the old lady's cash to protect himself. He tells it like he ain't ashamed, and finishes sayin', 'if you don't take care of yourself, nobody else will.'

"This talk makes the whole bunch wolfy. The passenger that's doin' the talkin' is for stoppin' the coach, and if there's a rope there'll be a hangin'. 'We dont need no rope; what's the matter with a lead rein? If he's as light in pounds as he is in principle, we'll slip a boulder in his pants to give him weight. This skunk is dirtier than airy hold-up on the road, and the sooner we pull this party, the better it suits me.'

"We're gettin' worked up on all this talk when the cowman that ain't turned a hair, says, 'If you gentlmen will let me play my hand out you'd find out who wins, but if you're bound to, go through with this hangin'.

"By this time, the old lady's beggin' for the cowman. She don't want to see him strung up, but thinks jail is strong enough. But these passengers are frothin' at the mouth, and it sure looks like the cowman's end is near. The driver has heard the story and stopped.

" 'Well,' says the old man, 'if you're bound to hang me,' (and he don't scare worth a dam) 'I'll slip my boots. I've been a gambler all my life' says he, draggin' off his right boot, 'but none of you shorthorns ever was; you never played nothin' but solitaire. This lady stakes me to fifty,' says he, 'and I always split my winnin's in the middle with them that stakes me.' And takin' a thousand dollars he's got tucked in his sock, he counts off five one-hundred-dollar bills, and hands them to the lady. 'That's yours,' says he.

"Nobody says nothin'. The old lady's shakin' hands, and, between sobs, thankin' this old cross-roader. Somebody tells the driver to drive on, and we're just pullin' into town when the man that's so strong for hangin' pulls a pint

We ain't gone five mile when the coach stops sudden an' a gent outside says, 'step out, folks, an'
keep your hands up while you're doin' it.

from his hip and says, 'To show you there's no hard feelin's, we'll all take a drink—barrin' the lady.' When the bottle comes back to its owner, its near dry, but before he empties it, he says, 'Here's to the gambler that pays his stakes!' Then he empties her and throws her out the window, and we all shake hands."

Adios

www.ingramcontent.com/pod-product-compliance
Lightning Source LLC
Chambersburg PA
CBHW080918190726
48293CB00011B/2691